WTW Supplemental Units 2-4

Someone Just Like Me

USE YOUR IMAGINATION

Someone Just Like Me

Story by Carol A. Marron

Illustrations by Cindy Wheeler

STECK-VAUGHN
COMPANY
A Subsidiary of National Education Corporation

To my Aunt Rose and Uncle Roy.

—C. M.

For Su and Jay, with special thanks.

—C. W.

First Steck-Vaughn Edition 1993
Published by Steck-Vaughn Company

Art Direction: Su Lund

1 2 3 4 5 6 7 8 9 W 97 96 95 94 93 92
ISBN 0-8114-8407-6

Carrie May and Nola Marie were twins. They had lived together all their lives and both were quite content.

But when Nola Marie
married and moved away, the
big, empty house made
Carrie May lonely.

"What I need is a roommate, Bixby. Someone to laugh with. Someone to talk to."

Carrie put her picture and a
notice in the Sunday paper.

Wanted: Cheerful woman
to live with same. Rent
will be *free* for the right
person—someone just like
me. Pets welcome.

Soon there was a crowd waiting outside Carrie May's door.

The first person in line had to be pushed from behind and pulled from in front.

"Oh dear," said Carrie May. "I am so thin and you are so plump. You can see we are not the same at all."

The next woman was very young.

"This is a wonderful house," she said. "All it needs is some new curtains, and some new furniture, and some new—"

"I'm sorry," Carrie May said. "I like my old curtains and my old furniture. After all, I'm pretty old myself."

The next person left a trail of mud on the carpet and spilled tea on her dress.

"Too messy," Carrie May whispered to Bixby. "I am too tidy to live with her."

Next came a sour-faced matron dragging a sour-faced dog.

"I don't like sunshine," she said, pulling down the shades. "I don't like music or flowers or children . . . and I especially don't like *cats*," she said, glaring at Bixby.

"And I don't like grouchy people," Carrie May said sweetly. "My ad called for a cheerful woman, and you won't do at all!"

The next woman came in and sat down without saying a word. She was so dull and plain, Carrie May couldn't think of a thing to say to her.

They stared at each other for several minutes. Then the stranger left as quietly as she had come.

"Really, Bixby, whoever lives here must be as clever and fancy as I am."

No sooner had the next woman walked through the door than Carrie May began to sneeze.

"I must be allergic to you," Carrie told her. "It could be your coat. I hate fur coats!

"Wait, Bixby! I love *your* fur coat. I love YOU!

"I guess I've never noticed
before how different we are.

"In fact, you're not like me *at all*. But we get along just fine.

"Perhaps I have been foolish, Bixby. Even Nola Marie wasn't *just* like me.

"If whoever comes next is willing, we will take a chance to get to know each other."

And things worked out very well. Carrie May and Bixby learned that when it comes to friends . . .

. . .little differences can be ignored.

ANTONYMS are words that have opposite meanings. An antonym for **fast** is **slow.** An antonym for **smooth** is **bumpy.** An antonym for **short** is **long.**

Did you notice the antonyms in this book? See how these words from the story have opposite meanings: **pushed** and **pulled, messy** and **tidy, grouchy** and **cheerful.** Can you find other examples in the story?

Antonyms — just one of many ways you can have fun with words.

Carol **Marron** is the author of several books for young readers. She was born in Minneapolis, Minnesota, and still lives there with her husband and three children.

Cindy **Wheeler** grew up in Alabama, Virginia, and North Carolina. After receiving a B.F.A. degree from Auburn University, the artist worked for a bookseller and for a publisher. Now she devotes her time to writing and illustrating children's books. Ms. Wheeler has written and illustrated *A Good Day, A Good Night* and a series of four books on a delightful cat named Marmalade. She also illustrated the 1980 edition of Charlotte Zolotow's classic *One Step, Two.* Ms. Wheeler lives on Glynwood Farm near Cold Spring, New York, with her husband and a black cat.